Secret
PRINCESSES

Special thanks to Linda Chapman
For two special sisters,
Emila and Olivia Crow

ORCHARD BOOKS

First published in Great Britain in 2016 by The Watts Publishing Group

1 3 5 7 9 10 8 6 4 2

Text copyright © Hothouse Fiction, 2016
Illustrations copyright © Orchard Books, 2016

A CIP catalogue record for this book
is available from the British Library.

ISBN 978 1 40834 211 4

Printed and bound in Great Britain by Clays Ltd, St Ives plc

The paper and board used in this book are made from wood from responsible sources.

Orchard Books
An imprint of
Hachette Children's Group
Part of The Watts Publishing Group Limited
Carmelite House
50 Victoria Embankment
London EC4Y 0DZ

An Hachette UK Company
www.hachette.co.uk
www.hachettechildrens.co.uk

Series created by Hothouse Fiction
www.hothousefiction.com

Snowflake
Sisters

ROSIE BANKS

Wishing Star Palace

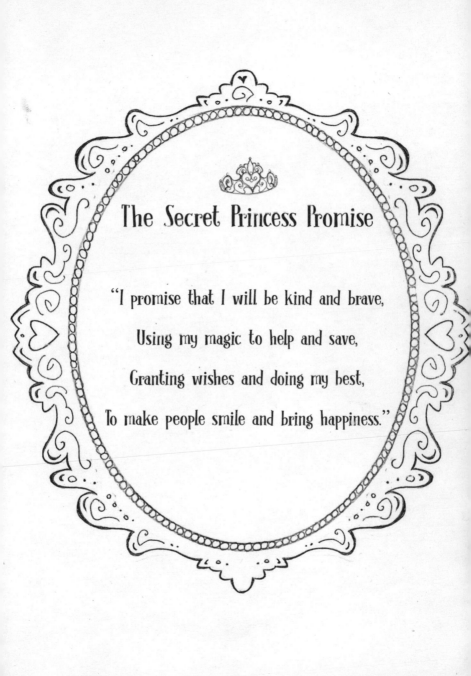

The Secret Princess Promise

"I promise that I will be kind and brave,

Using my magic to help and save,

Granting wishes and doing my best,

To make people smile and bring happiness."

# Story One

CHAPTER ONE

Christmas is Coming!

"*Jingle bells, jingle bells …* " Mia sang as she
sat on her bed, knitting a scarf. Happiness was
fizzing through her. It was Christmas – her
favourite time of year. She had decorated
her bedroom with paper chains and had
hung an orange studded with cloves from her
wardrobe door. It was making her room smell
sweet and spicy.

The scarf was going to be her mum's Christmas present. She couldn't wait to see her face when she unwrapped it on Christmas Day.

Just then, her bedroom door opened. Mia quickly pushed the scarf under her pillow.

But it wasn't Mum, it was her little sister, Elsie.

"Mia! Mia! Look what I made at playgroup!" Elsie said, skipping in, her blonde bunches bouncing. "But promise you won't tell Mummy. It's a surprise."

"I promise I won't tell," said Mia, with a smile. "What is it?"

Elsie opened her hand and showed Mia a necklace she had made from pasta shells painted gold. "Do you like it?" Elsie asked.

"It's great," Mia said enthusiastically.

13

"What are *you* giving Mummy?" Elsie asked.

Mia pulled the scarf out from under her pillow. "This."

"That's pretty," said Elsie, stroking it. "Are you making a scarf for Charlotte, too?"

Charlotte was Mia's best friend. She used to live nearby, but she and her family had moved to America earlier in the year. "No," said Mia. "It's really hot in California – far too hot to wear a scarf."

"Hot? At Christmas time?" said Elsie.

Mia nodded, thinking about the last time she had talked to Charlotte on the computer. Charlotte had been wearing shorts!

"So, what are you giving her?" asked Elsie.

"I'm knitting her a Christmas stocking," said Mia. "I'm going to put her favourite English sweets inside." She had an idea. "Why don't you make her a card? We could post it with my present. She'd love that."

"OK," said Elsie eagerly. "I'll go and get my crayons." She ran off.

Mia thought wistfully about Charlotte. They'd always done so much together at Christmas time. They'd gone shopping and carol singing, visited Santa at the shopping

centre, made Christmas decorations and baked
mince pies together. And of course, when
they were younger, they'd been in the school
Nativity play every year. It was so odd not
having her around at Christmas time.

She glanced down at the pendant shaped
like half a heart that hung from a golden chain
around her neck. Charlotte had the other half
of the heart. But they weren't just necklaces,
they were part of an amazing secret that the
girls shared.

Mia could still hardly believe it, but their
necklaces were magic! They transported her
and Charlotte to a beautiful place called
Wishing Star Palace. On their first visit, they
had discovered that they'd been chosen to

train as Secret Princesses – special people who could use magic to make wishes come true.

It was the most amazing thing that had ever happened to her! Best of all, she and Charlotte could still see each other lots!

Mia smiled and touched her necklace as she remembered the four Secret Princess adventures she and Charlotte had already shared. *We're so lucky*, she thought. It was the best feeling ever when she and Charlotte used magic to make someone happy.

A tingle ran across her fingertips and the pendant started to shine softly. Mia caught her breath as excitement rushed through her.

"I wish that I could see Charlotte!" she whispered quickly.

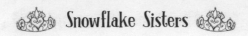

WHOOSH!

Golden light flooded out of the pendant,
swirling around her in a sparkling cloud. Mia
felt herself being lifted up and carried
away in a tunnel of light. For a moment,
she wondered what Elsie would say when she
came back into her bedroom but then
she remembered that time always stood still
while she and Charlotte were away on a
magical adventure.

Mia's feet touched the ground and she
opened her eyes. She was in the garden of
Wishing Star Palace, but she'd never seen
it look this beautiful. The lawn was covered
in a blanket of sparkling snow! The trees
had glittering icicles in all different colours

hanging from their branches and little robins flew about, singing sweetly.

Glancing down, Mia gave a little squeal of excitement. Her jeans and jumper had transformed into her beautiful golden princess dress and she was now wearing cosy lace-up boots. There was a white fake-fur wrap around her shoulders and fluffy mittens hanging on a silver ribbon around her neck. Putting her hand to her head, she felt her jewelled tiara there and glowed with pride.

She and Charlotte had earned their proper Secret Princess tiaras at the end of their last adventure, when they had passed the first stage of their princess training.

THUMP! A snowball hit her back. She spun round and saw Charlotte grinning at her. She was wearing her gorgeous pink princess dress and her sparkling diamond tiara was nestling in her curly brown hair. "Sorry! I couldn't resist. I've missed the snow so much!" Charlotte said.

Then she ran across the grass and flung her
arms round Mia.

They spun each other round, laughing.
"Doesn't it look beautiful!" said Mia.

Charlotte nodded.
"And guess what?
The icicles are all
different flavours!"
She broke a
pink one off and
handed it to Mia.
"I think this one is
watermelon."
Mia licked it.
The icicle tasted like strawberries to her, but
whatever flavour it was, it was delicious!

Charlotte broke a lime-green icicle off for herself. "Yum! Kiwi fruit!"

"Let's see if we can find the princesses," Mia said eagerly. "They must have brought us here for a reason."

"Maybe someone's wish needs granting!" Charlotte said.

"You don't suppose Princess Poison could be causing trouble again?" Mia asked as they hurried across the lawn.

Princess Poison was a Secret Princess who had turned bad. Instead of using her magic to help people, she used it to spoil wishes. Every time she stopped a wish being granted, she became more powerful. She, and her horrible servant, Hex, had tried to stop Charlotte and

Mia on all of their adventures so far.

"Well, if she is, we'll just have to stop her," Charlotte said firmly.

On their adventures, they had defeated Princess Poison four times. By doing so, they had repaired Wishing Star Palace, which had been damaged by the wishes Princess Poison had spoiled.

Now, as Wishing Star Palace loomed in front of them, Mia and Charlotte gasped out loud. Not only did it look shiny and new, it had been decorated for Christmas! The walls were covered with pretty, twinkling fairy lights and big, beautiful garlands of holly decorated the windowsills. A wreath made of sparkling golden stars hung on the front door.

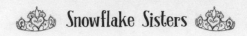

But it wasn't the gorgeous decorations that caught Mia's attention.

"Look!" she cried, pointing at the five animals frolicking in front of the palace. "Reindeer!"

CHAPTER TWO

A Mysterious Christmas Card

Mia and Charlotte hurried through the snow. The reindeer trotted over to greet them. Their coats were silky and their eyes were a deep, dark brown.

"Hello, there," murmured Mia, stroking the reindeer's soft fur.

"They're so gorgeous," said Charlotte.

Mia giggled as the reindeer's warm breath tickled her skin.

The reindeer seemed to like the fuss. They pushed their heads against the girls, snorting softly.

"Hello, girls!" A beautiful princess with short dark hair came out of the palace. She was wearing a bright blue dress and carrying a basket brimming with carrots.

"Princess Ella!" exclaimed Charlotte.

Princess Ella hugged them. "It's lovely to see you. We're decorating the palace for Christmas and thought you might like to help." She giggled as one of the reindeer tried to steal carrots from her basket. "Belle, stop it! Don't be naughty! I think I'd better feed them," she said.

"Would you like to help me, girls?"

They nodded eagerly. Princess Ella gave them both a handful of carrots. The reindeer crunched them up happily.

"Reindeer really love carrots," Princess Ella said, stroking the reindeer nearest to her. "Now, I imagine you two would like something to eat too? Let's go inside – Princess Sylvie has been baking some delicious Christmas treats."

The girls nodded eagerly. Princess Sylvie's special talent was baking and her cakes and biscuits were amazing – and magical!

Princess Ella led the way into the palace through the big front door. As she opened it, they stepped into the welcoming entrance hall. There was a fire roaring in the huge fireplace

and an enormous Christmas tree was waiting
to be decorated. The air was filled with the
delicious scent of gingerbread.

Charlotte took a deep breath.
"Mmmmmmm!" she
sighed happily.

"Everyone! Charlotte and Mia are here!"
Princess Ella called out.

The kitchen door opened and Princess Sylvie
came out carrying a golden
plate heaped with
gingerbread biscuits.
Her deep red hair
was piled on her head
and she was wearing a
green dress. She had a
golden cupcake pendant
around her neck.

Princess Ella's pendant
was a golden paw print.
Each princess's pendant
reflected her own talent.

Mia and Charlotte each had a matching half of a heart because they shared a very rare and special talent for friendship.

"Hello, girls," Princess Sylvie said, beaming at them. "Would you like some gingerbread?"

"Ooh, yes please," said Mia, taking a gingerbread lady. She felt a little bit disappointed as she looked at it. She had expected something amazing, but the gingerbread figure was totally plain, with no decoration at all. But Mia didn't want to upset Princess Sylvie so she said, "Thank you. They look delicious!"

Princess Sylvie flicked her wand and Mia gasped. The gingerbread figure started to change! Long blonde hair, just like her own, appeared in icing, and so did a gold dress and fur cape. Boots appeared on the gingerbread figure's feet, a half-heart shaped pendant around its neck and a tiara in its hair – all made from icing.

"It … it looks just like me!" Mia stammered in amazement.

Princess Sylvie's eyes twinkled. "Well, I did add a teaspoon of magic to the recipe."

"Mine looks just like me now too!" said Charlotte, holding up her gingerbread figure, which now had dark skin, a pink dress and curly brown hair made from icing.

"Try them," said Princess Sylvie.

Charlotte looked shocked. "I couldn't eat it. It's too special!"

Princess Ella smiled. "Why don't you hang them on the tree instead?"

The girls ran to hang the gingerbread princesses on the tree. When they came back, Princess Sylvie offered them a plate of gingerbread stars decorated with pretty glittery icing.

"Yum!" said Mia, as she bit into the biscuit. "This is delicious. Please may I have the recipe?"

"Of course," said Princess Sylvie, taking a piece of paper out of her pocket and touching it with her wand. A recipe appeared on it. "You won't be able to use a teaspoon of magic outside Wishing Star Palace, of course, but if you follow the rest of the recipe, it will still make great-tasting gingerbread!"

Another door opened and in came a princess in a red dress, carrying a box of Christmas decorations. She had a musical note pendant on her necklace.

"Alice!" cried the girls.

Alice De Silver – or Princess Alice as she was known at Wishing Star Palace – was a famous pop star. She had once been the girls' babysitter. It had been Alice who had given

them their magical
necklaces and
helped them
become Secret
Princess
trainees.

"Hello,
you two," she
said, putting
the box down
and hugging them.

"You're just in time to
help me decorate the tree. Now, let me see ...
Hmm, yes, it definitely needs some tinsel!"
She waved her wand. Golden sparkles shot out
and flew around the tree before settling on the

branches and turning into beautiful garlands of glittering gold tinsel.

"And some icicles!" said Alice, waving her wand again. This time silver sparkles shot out and zoomed around the tree. The girls laughed in delight as the sparkles landed on the branches and formed delicate glass icicles.

"And definitely some candy canes!" said Princess Ella, waving her wand.

Red and white sparkles flew out and

turned into pretty stripy
candy canes.

"I like decorating the
Secret Princess way!"
said Charlotte.

"Granting people's
Christmas wishes
makes Christmas
here at Wishing
Star Palace
magical," Alice
explained.
She opened
the box
she had
brought in.

"Just the baubles to go now." Inside were rows of glass baubles, each a different shape. There was a musical note, a paw print, a cupcake …

"They're like the pendants on our necklaces!" Mia realised.

Alice smiled. "There's one for each of us." She handed Mia and Charlotte the two half-heart shaped ornaments. "Why don't you girls hang yours next to each other?" she suggested. "Because Friendship Princesses are always close at heart."

Charlotte and Mia ran
to hang their baubles
on a branch.

Princess Ella
and Princess
Sylvie started
to hang up
ornaments too,
and then some
of the other
princesses came
in from the gardens.

As they all worked together to decorate the
hall, Alice sang her latest hit and everyone
joined in. They had just finished and were
standing back to admire the hall when an

envelope fell through the letter flap and landed on the doormat.

"Our first Christmas card!" said Princess Sophie. "I wonder who it's from?"

Charlotte ran over and picked it up. "Should I open it?"

The princesses nodded. Charlotte opened the envelope. Inside was a card with a picture of a Christmas tree on the front.

But suddenly the picture started to change. The Christmas tree's needles blackened and fell off, the ornaments vanished until all that was left was a tree with bare, drooping branches.

"What's happened to it?" Charlotte said in dismay.

She opened the card and a puff of green smoke swirled out.

There was a message inside written in spiky green handwriting. Charlotte read it out.

"Christmas comes but once a year,
Bringing gifts and much good cheer,
But I'll spoil wishes for everyone,
So in the palace there'll be no fun!
From, Princess Poison."

All the princesses gasped in dismay.

"Princess Poison is going to try and ruin people's Christmas wishes!" Princess Sylvie exclaimed. "Oh no! How could she?"

"That's so mean!" said Princess Evie. "She knows spoiling wishes will spoil Christmas magic here, too."

Charlotte lifted her chin. "Whatever she tries, we'll stop her!"

Mia nodded firmly. Her heart was racing at the thought of facing Princess Poison again,

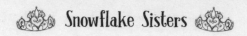

but she knew that Charlotte was right. "There's no way we'll let Princess Poison ruin anyone's Christmas wish," she declared. "No way at all!"

CHAPTER THREE
Santa's Grotto

All the princesses gathered in an anxious group. "Charlotte and Mia are right. We won't let Princess Poison spoil anyone's Christmas," said Princess Ella.

"Oh my gosh!" Mia cried suddenly. "Look!" All the baubles on the tree had suddenly started to glow.

"Someone's made a wish," said Alice.

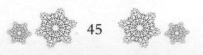

"But not just any wish – it must be a special Christmas wish!"

"Who's making the wish?" said Mia.

Alice went and picked up a bauble, and they peered into it. A picture of two girls had appeared in its shiny surface. They looked very similar and both had long black hair and almond-shaped eyes.

"There are two girls," Mia said.

"Maybe they're sisters?" Charlotte wondered.

"Two girls means it's the perfect job for our two trainee Friendship Princesses." Alice told them. "Will you help make their Christmas wish come true?"

"Yes!" they said eagerly.

The Secret Princesses cheered.

"You'll have extra wishes to use because there are two girls to help," said Alice. "Instead of the normal three wishes, you'll have six."

"Please be careful!" said Princess Sylvie anxiously. "If Princess Poison spoils a special Christmas wish, she'll get even more powerful."

"We're more than a match for her!" said
Charlotte. She took Mia's hand and squeezed
it. "Are you ready for another adventure?"

"Oh yes!" Mia breathed, taking her hand.
The baubles glowed even more brightly and
two names appeared in the bauble the girls
were holding.

"Say the girls'
names," Alice
instructed them.

Mia read
one out.
"Holly."

Charlotte
read out the
other. "Ivy."

Dazzling golden light shone out of the
baubles, sweeping them away. Mia clung
to Charlotte's hand as they spun round and
round.

THUMP!

Their feet hit the ground. Christmas music
was playing and they could smell perfume.

Opening their eyes, they saw that they were inside a busy department store, outside Santa's grotto. There was a long queue of people waiting to go and see Santa but, thanks to the way the magic worked, no one seemed to notice their sudden appearance. The magic had also changed them back into normal

clothes so that they would fit in with the crowds of Christmas shoppers.

"OK, so where are Holly and Ivy?" Mia whispered.

Charlotte looked around. "There!" she whispered, nodding to the front of the queue. The two girls were waiting patiently together, the older girl holding the younger girl's hand.

Suddenly a little, round man dressed in an

elf costume came barging

past everyone in the

queue. His pointed

green hat was

covering his face

and his costume

strained over

his large tummy.

"Sorry!" he said,

stopping in front of the

grotto door. "Santa's grotto

is shut now." But he didn't sound sorry at all.

In fact, he gave a mean snigger as he pulled

the door shut and turned a sign from 'Open' to

'Closed'. "Now go away!"

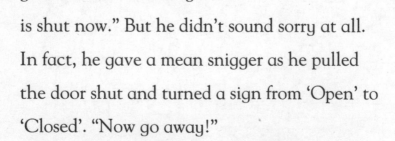

Holly and Ivy looked at each other in dismay. "But we've been waiting ages," said the older girl. "And my little sister, Ivy, really wants to see Santa."

"Well she can't, so you'd better just buzz off!" said the little man rudely. "Go on! Shoo!" He flapped his hands at them.

Some of the parents started turning away, muttering angrily. Ivy looked like she was going to cry.

"That's really strange," said Charlotte.

"Why didn't that elf come from *inside* Santa's grotto?"

Mia's attention was on Holly, who was pleading with the man. "My sister has a wish she really wants to tell Santa," Holly was saying. "It's really important—"

"Get lost!" shouted the elf.

"He's being really mean," said Mia. "Charlotte, you don't think it's … " The little man threw his hat back and Mia gasped. "Charlotte! It's Hex!"

"I knew there was something odd about him!" Charlotte whispered. "Princess Poison must be behind this. She's trying to stop Holly and Ivy's wish from coming true. Well, we'll just see about that!"

"What can we do?" whispered Mia as everyone started to troop off. Holly was crouching down, comforting Ivy. Hex gave them a triumphant look and marched away.

Charlotte's eyes lit up with an idea. "Hex isn't the only one who can disguise himself! We can too – we just need to use a little bit of Wish Magic!"

She pulled Mia behind a display and took her pendant out from under her shirt. Mia had no idea what Charlotte's plan was, but she trusted her completely. They touched their glowing pendants together so they formed a whole heart.

Mia looked at Charlotte. What was she going to wish for?

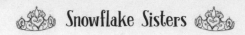

"I know how we can help Holly and Ivy see Santa," Charlotte grinned. "I wish we were dressed up as Christmas elves!"

CHAPTER FOUR

Making Wishes

FLASH!

Light blazed out from the pendants. Mia and
Charlotte gasped in delight as elf costumes
appeared over their clothes! They were each
wearing a little green hat with a bell and a
green dress with a red belt.

"This is perfect!" said Charlotte, looking at
her costume in delight. "Come on!"

Mia ran after her as Charlotte raced to the
grotto. Holly and Ivy were about to leave.
"Don't go!" Charlotte cried. "You can come
on in!" She turned the sign back to 'Open' and
opened the door. Mia looked inside. There was
a corridor decorated with fake snow, tinsel
and holly and a sign with an arrow saying

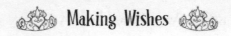
'This way to the North Pole!'

"Oh, wow! Really?" said Holly. She took Ivy's hand. "Did you hear that, Ivy? We *can* see Santa after all!"

The little girl's face lit up. "Can we go in now?" she asked.

"Yes. Come on!" said Charlotte brightly.

The girls led the way down the corridor.

"You're much nicer than that other elf!" Ivy said to her. "What's your name?"

"I'm Charlotte and this is Mia," said Charlotte.

"I'm Ivy Lee," said the little girl. "And this is my sister, Holly." She took Charlotte's hand and skipped beside her.

Mia smiled. "Have you been waiting long to see Santa?" she asked, turning to Holly.

Holly nodded. "Mum went off to do some shopping. I'm supposed to ring her when we've seen him."

They reached an archway with a curtain of snowflakes. Charlotte pulled the curtain aside and they all saw Santa sitting in a big

armchair beside a Christmas tree. He had a
huge bag of presents beside him.

"Santa!" gasped Ivy.

"Hello," he said with a warm smile. "Come in, my dears. I was beginning to wonder where everyone was."

"A mean elf tried to shut the grotto," Ivy told him.

Santa looked surprised. "How strange," he said. He patted a bench beside him. "Now why don't you two sit down and tell me your names?"

"I'm Holly and this is Ivy," said Holly.

Santa chuckled. "What lovely Christmassy names you have!"

"Our parents chose them for us because they love Christmas so much," said Holly.

"Mummy's sad because Daddy's away at the moment with work," said Ivy. She edged closer.

"Santa, Holly and I have got a Christmas wish we'd like to make."

"Ho, ho, ho, maybe I can help with that." Santa chuckled kindly. "What is it?"

Mia and Charlotte both listened closely.

"We wish we could have a happy family Christmas," said Ivy.

"But surely you will have that, won't you?" said Santa.

"We're not sure," said Ivy. "Mummy's been really busy because Daddy's away."

"He's been working abroad," Holly put in. "He might not get home in time for the carol concert tonight in the town square. We're both singing in it."

"We just wish that we could have a really happy Christmas all together," said Ivy.

"What a lovely wish," said Santa. "Well, who knows, my dears, maybe it will be granted. I really do hope so."

Mia and Charlotte's eyes met. They both hoped so, too!

Mia thought quickly. How could they make

Holly and Ivy's wish come true? They couldn't grant one big wish to make sure the family *did* have a great Christmas. Their magic wasn't powerful enough for that. But they could make five more smaller wishes that would help in some way ...

"Here's a little present for you," Santa went on. He rummaged in his sack and gave Ivy and Holly a present each. "I'm sure I'll be dropping lots more down your chimney on Christmas Eve! Goodbye for now."

The girls said goodbye. Mia led the way out of the grotto. She was still thinking hard about how they could help. They opened the door of the grotto and stepped out into the busy department store again.

"Thank you for taking us to see Santa," said Ivy, turning and giving Charlotte a hug. "I hope he makes our Christmas wish come true."

"Hopefully he will," said Charlotte, winking at Mia. "You never know what Santa can—" She broke off with a gasp as a familiar figure in an elf suit jumped out from behind a display of Christmas decorations and grabbed the presents from the girls.

"Wait!" cried Holly. "Come back!"

But Hex charged away with the gifts. Ivy burst into tears. "That mean elf stole my present!"

"Don't worry, we'll get them back!" cried Charlotte. She sprinted after Hex with Mia hot on her heels.

"Stop!" Charlotte shouted, not caring that people were looking at them.

Hex chortled. "Can't catch me!" he shouted over his shoulder. He darted round a rail of clothes and bashed into a display mannequin, sending it flying. A shop assistant shrieked. Charlotte and Mia leapt over the fallen dummy. Hex was heading for some stairs, but they couldn't let him get away!

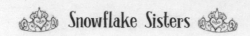

He leapt down the stairs at a time, pushing shoppers out of the way.

"The banisters, Mia!" gasped Charlotte.

Reaching the banister, she threw her leg over it and slid down. She leapt off at the end just in front of Hex.

"Oh no, you don't!" he cried, dodging her

and heading into the toy department.

Charlotte grabbed a handful of balls from a nearby display and threw them at him. *THUMP! THUD!* They hit his head, knocking his hat off.

"Hey! Ouch!" he cried.

Mia grabbed a child's umbrella. "Corner him, Charlotte!"

Hex darted down an aisle but it was a dead

end with just a changing room at the bottom. He pulled the curtain back to reveal an empty cubicle and mirror, but there was no escape. The girls had him trapped!

"Give those presents back," Charlotte said.

"Ivy's very upset," said Mia, holding the umbrella like a weapon.

"Oh, all right," Hex said sulkily, throwing them down on the ground. "You can have the stupid presents."

There was a bright green flash and the girls gasped as an image of Princess Poison appeared in the changing-room mirror. She was wearing a long green gown and had her sharp crown perched on top of her black hair, which had an ice-blonde streak. Her eyes glittered nastily.

"Yes, you can have the presents!" she snapped. "But they won't do any good. I'm going to make sure that the girls' Christmas wish doesn't come true – so the Secret Princesses' Christmas will be ruined too." Her lips curved in a sneer. "Come, Hex!

She pointed her wand and then she and Hex vanished in a puff of smoke.

Mia and Charlotte stared at each other. "What are we going to do?" said Mia.

"Ignore her," said Charlotte fiercely. She ran to the presents and picked them up. "Let's take these back to Holly and Ivy and see if we can help make their wish come true."

They quickly took off their elf costumes, then ran back through the department store to where Holly was comforting Ivy. A woman had joined them. Mia guessed it was the girls' mum because she had the same straight, dark hair and almond-shaped eyes. "I can't believe one of the elves stole your presents," she was saying. "That's dreadful."

"He was horrible, Mummy," said Ivy.

"I imagine he was just pretending to be one of the elves," said her mum.

"He was," said Charlotte, hurrying over. "But we caught up with him and made him give the presents back. Here." She and Mia handed Holly and Ivy the gifts.

Ivy's tears dried up instantly. "My present!" she cried. "Thank you!"

"This is Charlotte and Mia, Mum," said Holly, seeing her mum give Charlotte and Mia a curious look. "They're elves in the grotto."

"Just sometimes. We're done now," said Charlotte quickly.

"Thank you so much, girls," said Mrs Lee. "We were about to go home for lunch. Would you like to join us?"

"Oh, yes please!" said Mia. That would give them the perfect chance to try and grant Holly and Ivy's wishes!

"That would be great!" said Charlotte.

Mrs Lee smiled. "Wonderful. I'll just check that's OK with your parents. Where are they?"

Mia and Charlotte exchanged anxious looks. "Um ..." said Charlotte.

Mia's mind raced desperately. Now what were they going to do?

CHAPTER FIVE

An Unexpected Arrival

"Ah, there you are, girls!" Hearing a familiar voice, Mia and Charlotte swung round.

"Prin—" Mia broke off as Charlotte elbowed her in the side.

"Ella!" Charlotte exclaimed.

Princess Ella was walking through the shop towards them. She was dressed in jeans and a jumper and looked like a mum or older sister.

"I was just starting to wonder where you'd got to," she said, coming over. She gave Holly and Ivy and their mum a warm smile. "Hi, I'm Ella. I hope the girls aren't bothering you."

"Not at all," said Mrs Lee. "In fact, Holly and Ivy have just asked if they can come back for lunch. Would that be OK? Our house is just down the road."

"Please can we go?" Mia said to Ella.

"Of course you can," said Ella. "That's very kind of you," she said to Mrs Lee. "I've got so much to get done this afternoon. What time should I come and pick them up?"

"Well, Holly and Ivy are free until the carol concert in the town square this evening," said Mrs Lee. "The girls can stay until then."

"Perfect! I can meet them at the concert," said Ella. "See you later, girls!"

"Bye!" called Charlotte and Mia.

"Come along then," said Mrs Lee. "Let's go."

Charlotte and Mia fell into step beside Holly and Ivy. Ivy held Charlotte's hand. "I'm glad you're coming back with us," she said happily. "What should we do when we get home?"

"We still need to get a Christmas present for Mum," Holly reminded her. "We didn't find anything we liked at the shops," she told Charlotte and Mia.

Mia thought about Elsie making a necklace for their mum. "You don't have to buy a present. You could make one. I'm sure that would make your mum really happy."

She suddenly remembered the recipe in her pocket. Lowering her voice, she said, "How about baking her some yummy gingerbread?"

"Oh yes! Mum loves gingerbread," said Holly. "Ivy, we could do that when we get home – and make her a Christmas card too."

Ivy skipped in delight. "Let's use lots of glitter!"

Mrs Lee looked round with a smile. "What are you all whispering about?"

"Just deciding what we want to do at home," said Ivy. "Can we do some baking?"

"Of course, as long as you don't make too much mess," said her mum. "I've got so much to do – presents to wrap, cards to write and the tree to decorate." She ran a hand through her hair. "I don't know how I'm going to get everything done before your dad comes home tonight – if he gets home by then," she added with an anxious glance at the heavy grey sky. "There's more snow forecast. He's worried he's going to be delayed."

"I hope not," said Holly. "I really want him to come to the carol concert tonight." She turned to Charlotte and Mia. "I'm singing a solo in *Silent Night*."

The Lees' house was just a short walk from the shops. The girls had fun scooping snow off walls to make snowballs that they threw at each other. As soon as they got inside the warm house, they went into the cosy kitchen. It had a big wooden table in the middle, red and white polka dot curtains and a big pine dresser with brightly coloured plates on it. "Holly and Ivy know where the baking things are," Mrs Lee said as she turned the oven on to heat up. "Call me when you're ready and I'll put it in the oven."

"Thanks, Mum," said Holly. Holly took some cookery books down from the dresser. "We'd better find a recipe."

"No need to do that," said Mia. She pulled

the recipe Princess Sylvie had given her out of her pocket. "I have one here!"

Holly grinned. "Then let's get started."

Mia started to read out the ingredients. "OK, it says we need flour and butter and …"

She broke off as she saw a flash of green light from outside the window. "What was that?" she said.

"What was what?" said Charlotte.

"That weird light."

"I didn't see anything," said Holly.

Mia peered out the window. The garden was empty, the bushes and trees coated in thick snow. Maybe she'd just imagined it. None of the others seemed to have noticed anything strange.

"Sorry, I thought I saw something," she said.
"OK, where was I?"

She continued to read out the ingredients.
Holly and Ivy got everything out of the
cupboards and started to measure and mix.

Holly put some Christmas music on, too. Soon they were rolling out the dough and cutting out Christmassy gingerbread shapes while singing along to Christmas songs. They made angels and Christmas trees, bells and stars and reindeer. Then they put them on a baking tray

and called Mrs Lee down to help put them in the oven.

"It's a shame Mum has to see," Holly whispered to the others.

"Don't look!" Ivy told her mum.

Mrs Lee laughed and shaded her face with her oven glove. "I can't see anything, I promise," she said as she carefully put the tray in the oven.

As they tidied the table and washed up the mixing bowl, the kitchen started to fill with the delicious scent of baking gingerbread.

"Yum!" said Ivy, sniffing. "Can we take them out and eat them?"

"Ivy! They're for Mum," scolded Holly. She grinned. "But I'm sure there'll be some spare."

"While we're waiting for them to bake, we could make some Christmas cards," said Mia. "Have you got any craft materials?"

"Ooh yes. Lots," said Ivy.

Leaving the gingerbread to bake, they all headed through to the playroom. Ivy and Holly made a Christmas card for their mum with a Christmas tree on the front decorated with paint and green glitter, while Mia and Charlotte made long paper chains to decorate the lounge.

"This is so much fun!" said Holly happily as she and Ivy stood their card up to let it dry.

"The gingerbread must be done by now," said Mia, excitedly.

They opened the door and smelled burning.

"Ew!" said Ivy, wrinkling her nose. "What is that horrible smell?"

"Oh no! It must be the gingerbread!" gasped Holly in dismay.

They ran into the kitchen and gasped. It was filled with a huge cloud of black smoke.

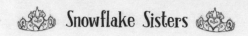

Holly ran over to the oven and opened it.
"Look!" she gasped.

Every single piece of gingerbread was burnt
black and horrible!

CHAPTER SIX
An Unwelcome Guest

"What happened?" said Holly as they all stared at the burnt gingerbread.

Ivy started to cry.

Mia checked the oven controls and frowned. "Someone must have turned the heat up. It's much too hot."

"But who did that?" said Holly.

Just then, Mia caught sight of the recipe

Princess Sylvie had given her. The writing on it had been replaced with three words scrawled in green ink: *Ha! Ha! Ha!*

Her heart plummeted. "I think I know who," she said, picking the paper up and showing it to Charlotte.

"Oh no," Charlotte groaned.

"What are we going to do about Mummy's gingerbread?" Ivy sobbed. "We've used up all the ingredients so we can't make any more!"

"Don't worry," Mia said, reaching out and taking her hand. "Charlotte and I can fix this. I promise."

"But how?" asked Holly.

Mia looked at Charlotte, who nodded. It was time to tell Holly and Ivy the truth.

"Charlotte and I have a secret," Mia said. "We're training to become Secret Princesses."

"Princesses!" breathed Ivy, her tears drying up as she stared at them.

"What do you mean?" said Holly incredulously.

"We're a bit like fairy godmothers," explained Charlotte. "We use magic to make wishes come true."

"When the grotto was shut, we made a wish to be elves so we could help Ivy see Santa," said Mia.

Holly gaped at them. "Oh! I thought that you were a bit young to be elves."

Ivy frowned. "If you're princesses, where are your tiaras?"

"We keep them at the palace," Charlotte explained. "No one except the people we're helping can know about the magic."

Ivy's eyes widened. "Really? Well, if you can grant wishes, can I have a unicorn?" she said. "And a ballet tutu and ...?"

Charlotte grinned. "I'm afraid not. We can only use our magic help make your Christmas wish come true – to have a happy family Christmas."

"And we can start by wishing that the gingerbread for your mum is as yummy as it should be!" said Mia, with a grin. "Watch this!"

She and Charlotte pulled their pendants out from under their tops. The half hearts were glowing brightly. They brought them together, making a perfect heart.

"I wish that the gingerbread could be perfect!" said Mia.

FLASH!

The burnt gingerbread in the oven vanished

– as did the smoke. In its place, a gorgeous gingerbread palace appeared on the kitchen table. It was drizzled with white icing and its

turrets were decorated with hundreds of sweets and silver balls. It looked just like Wishing Star Palace!

"Oh … my …

goodness," said Holly faintly, while Ivy clapped in delight and jumped up and down. "You really *can* do magic!"

Charlotte and Mia nodded.

"Mummy's going to love it!" squealed Ivy. "Thank you!" She hugged Mia and Charlotte.

"I'll hide it in my bedroom until Christmas Day." Holly said. She hurried upstairs and when she returned she said, "Let's hang up the paper chains you made."

In the lounge, there was a Christmas tree by the window, but its branches were bare. On the floor were three cardboard boxes overflowing with decorations and baubles.

"Can we put some tinsel up as well as the paper chains?" said Ivy, draping some over her head. "I love tinsel!"

"Why don't we decorate the whole room?" said Charlotte. "That will help your mum out."

"Good idea," said Holly. "I'll put on some more Christmas music."

As she fiddled with the music player,

Charlotte went over to Mia.

"We need to be on our guard," she said to Mia in a low voice. "Princess Poison must have used her magic to turn the oven up."

"I know. That flash of green light I saw must have been her," Mia whispered back anxiously.

They all worked together to decorate the room. They hung up the paper chains and tinsel, wound strings of fairy lights around the Christmas tree and hung pretty baubles from its branches. By the time they had finished, the lounge looked beautiful.

"Now, we just need to find the star to put on the top of the tree," said Holly, starting to hunt through the decoration box. "It should be in here somewhere. Oh." Her face fell as she pulled out a bent golden star. "It's broken."

"Maybe we can make another one," suggested Mia.

Just then, the doorbell went. Mia looked out

through the window. "It's a delivery person,"
she said. A delivery person in a green uniform
stood in the porch, holding a huge stack of
brightly wrapped gifts.

There were so many
boxes Mia couldn't
even see the
person behind
them!

"Can you get
the door please,
girls?" Mrs Lee
called down
from upstairs.

Holly hurried into
the hall.

"It's a special delivery for the Lee family,"
Mia heard a woman's voice say. "Where would
you like me to put these boxes?"

"Could you bring them through to the
lounge, please?" Holly said. "We can put them
under the tree."

Holly led the delivery person into the room.

"Presents!" breathed Ivy, her eyes widening.

"I'll just put them here," said the lady. "Oh,
and I have one more present for you." She
sniggered. It wasn't a nice laugh.

Mia frowned. "What sort of present?" she
asked as the tall lady dumped the presents on
the carpet.

The delivery lady swung round, swishing her
long dark hair with a ice-blonde streak in it.

"My favourite type of present – one that makes people unhappy!" she cried.

"Princess Poison!" gasped Mia and Charlotte.

Princess Poison cackled nastily. "Yes, it's me!"

"But who are you?" demanded Holly in confusion. Ivy hid behind her, peeking out at the mean princess.

"Someone who's going to make sure you have a *miserable* Christmas!" cried Princess Poison, pulling a wand out of her delivery uniform's pocket.

She swung it round the room and called out a spell before Charlotte or Mia could stop her.

"Tinsel turn to shreds,
Needles drop off the tree
Banish all festive fun,
Bring Christmas misery!"

Green light exploded out of the tip of her wand and hit the Christmas tree. Needles dropped from the branches. One by one, the fairy lights all popped and went out.

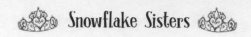

The presents Princess Poison had brought in vanished, leaving just crumpled wrapping paper behind.

"No!" gasped Holly. Ivy started to cry.

"Princess Poison, you can't do this!" cried Charlotte.

Princess Poison smirked. "Oh, I think you'll find I can!" She swept towards the door. "Merry Christmas, everyone!" With a gleeful laugh, she left, slamming the door behind her.

CHAPTER SEVEN
Christmas Magic

Ivy sobbed. "That lady ruined all our decorations."

"She did it using magic," said Holly, looking at Mia and Charlotte. "Who is she?"

"Her name's Princess Poison," said Charlotte. She quickly told Ivy and Holly all about the wicked princess.

"She wants to spoil Christmas," said Mia.

"But don't worry, we can fix the decorations – with magic!" She picked up her pendant.

Just then Mrs Lee called down the stairs. "I'll be with you in a minute, girls. You must be ready for lunch by now!"

"Quick!" said Holly, looking around at the bare branches of the Christmas tree and heaps of crumpled wrapping paper on the floor. "Mum will be so upset if she comes in and sees this."

Mia and Charlotte put their pendants together. "We wish for the lounge to be beautifully decorated!" said Charlotte quickly.

Light streamed out of the pendants. As it flooded around the room, the magic started to work! First the tree was transformed, complete with new fairy lights, baubles and tinsel.

Colourful paper chains appeared on the walls
and pretty stockings magically appeared over
the fireplace, which was decorated with candles
and holly. Pretty glass bowls filled with sweets
and nuts appeared on the window ledges and a

string of golden stars decorated the bookcase.
Soon it looked even better than it had before.

Holly beamed and hugged Charlotte and
Mia. "Oh wow! Mum will love it. Thank you!"

"Mum will love what?" said Mrs Lee,

suddenly appearing in the doorway. She gasped. "Oh my goodness – look at this room!" She stared around the room, astonished. "How did you girls manage to do it all?"

Holly and Ivy looked at Charlotte and Mia.

"By all working together," said Mia quickly.

"And we've got a Christmas card for you, too," said Ivy. She ran through to the playroom and came back with the glittery card. "Holly and I made it together," she said proudly, as her mum opened the card and looked inside. "There are lots of kisses at the bottom because we love you very much."

Mrs Lee sank down on the arm of one of the chairs and bit her lip. Tears welled in her eyes.

"Why are you crying, Mummy?" Ivy asked

anxiously, going over to her. "You're not sad, are you?"

Mrs Lee sniffed and then smiled through her tears. "No, I'm not." She drew Ivy into a hug and held her other arm out to Holly, who joined in with the cuddle. "I can't tell you how worried I've been about how much I still had to do. So to find that you've been so helpful … it's just incredible. I'm not crying because I'm sad, Ivy. I'm crying because you've made me so happy!"

There was a bright flash of light by the Christmas tree. Mrs Lee didn't notice it, but all the girls did. The fairy lights suddenly started to twinkle even more brightly and a beautiful princess in a long white dress appeared at the top of the tree. Mia squeezed Charlotte's hand in delight. The girls' wish was starting to come true!

"Oh dear, I'm going to have to get a tissue," said Mrs Lee, laughing as she wiping her eyes. She hurried from the room.

"There's an angel on the tree top," Holly whispered, staring at it. "It just appeared."

"It's not an angel," said Ivy, her eyes shining. "It's a princess, isn't it?" she said, turning to Mia and Charlotte. "A Secret Princess!"

"It is," said Charlotte with a smile.

Ivy hugged her. "Thank you!"

Mia turned to Holly. "I'm so glad your mum is happy. We're one step closer to giving you the happy family Christmas you wanted. Next, we'll try and make sure your dad gets home for the carol concert, too."

"Oh, I really hope he does," said Holly. "I want to see him so much."

"We'll do our best," promised Charlotte.

"Girls," Mrs Lee called from the kitchen. "Come and have some lunch!"

They ran through to the kitchen and helped get out all the lunch things. There were turkey and cranberry sandwiches, crisps, nuts and mince pies. It was delicious! Mrs Lee even found some crackers for them to pull.

Charlotte read out the joke from hers. "What do you get if you cross Santa with a duck?"

"What?" asked everyone.

Charlotte grinned. "Christmas Quackers!"

They all groaned.

"These jokes are awful," said Holly.

"I like them," said Charlotte, gathering together all the jokes. "Here's another. How do snowmen get around?"

"How?" said Ivy.

"On *icicles*, of course!"

Everyone groaned again.

"And how about this one—" said Charlotte.

"No, stop!" said Mia, with a giggle.
"Charlotte will tell jokes all afternoon if you let
her," she told the others.

Mrs Lee smiled round at them. "Well, fun
though this is, I'd better finish wrapping some
presents. Now that's a task you *really* can't
help me with," she said, looking at Ivy and
Holly with a twinkle in her eyes. "What are
you four going to do?"

"We'll clear up," Holly told her. "Then we
can decide."

They all got up and started clearing away
the plates and cutlery.

"I hope Princess Poison doesn't come back and try to deliver any more horrible presents this afternoon," Mia said to Charlotte.

"We'll be ready for her if she does," said Charlotte. "We're not going to let her ruin anyone's Christmas."

"No, we'll grant Holly and Ivy's wish to have a happy family Christmas," said Mia. "No matter what Hex and Princess Poison do."

Charlotte grinned. "One thing's for sure – it's going to be a *magical* afternoon!"

Story Two

CHAPTER ONE
Fun in the Snow

"It's snowing again!" Ivy said, kneeling on a chair and looking out of the window. "Come on, let's go and play!"

"We can have a snowball fight!" suggested Charlotte.

"And make snow angels," said Mia.

"And a snowman!" Ivy piped up.

"I'll just check with Mum that it's OK for us

to go the woods at the end of our road," said
Holly. She went upstairs and came back a few
minutes later. "She said it's fine as long as
I take my phone and we aren't out too long."

All the girls raced to put on their hats,
gloves and
scarves, then
headed
outside.
The frosty
air stung
their cheeks
and the snow
crunched
under their
feet.

"I love the snow," said Ivy, dancing around.

"Me too, usually," said Holly quietly, gazing up at the sky. "But not today."

"What's wrong?" Mia asked her gently.

"I don't want the snow to stop Dad from getting back for the carol concert," Holly said, sighing. "I really want him to hear my solo. And after the choir sings the lights on the town's Christmas tree are switched on, and Dad loves that bit. It's always one of the nicest parts of Christmas."

"It sounds lovely," said Mia. She could tell how much it meant to Holly.

"Look! Look! There's a robin!" said Ivy,
pointing to a robin perched on a wall close by.
"Isn't it fat?"

"It's not fat, it's
just fluffing up its
feathers to keep out
the cold," said Mia.
"Lots of birds do that."

"I didn't know that," said Holly, impressed.

"Mia knows loads of facts about birds and
animals," said Charlotte. "She loves them."
She grinned. "Bet you don't know the answer
to this though, Mia. What do you call a bad-
mannered deer?"

"What?" said Mia.

"*Rude*-olph, of course!"

Even Holly smiled. Mia threw a snowball at Charlotte, who ran off laughing. Ivy ran after her.

"Let's go to the pond!" Ivy called to Charlotte. "We usually go skating on it with Daddy when it freezes."

Mia and Holly hurried after the sisters and caught up with them beside a large frozen pond.

"I wish we could go skating," said Ivy.

"It's covered with snow and we haven't got skates," Holly pointed out. She sighed. "Oh, I wish Dad was here."

Ivy looked sad. "I miss him, too."

Mia pulled Charlotte to one side. "The girls' wish for a happy family Christmas won't be granted if their dad isn't here," she said.

Charlotte thought for a moment. "I know!" she said suddenly. "Why don't we try wishing for him to appear."

"Do you think we have enough magic to do that?" wondered Mia.

"There's only one way to find out," Charlotte said.

As Holly and Ivy watched hopefully, the girls put their glowing pendants together. "We wish for Holly and Ivy's dad to arrive," Charlotte said.

But nothing magical happened. Holly and Ivy's faces fell.

Shaking her head, Mia said, "Well, it was worth a try." She looked at Holly and Ivy,

who were gazing worriedly
up at the snowflakes.
"We really need
to cheer them up,"
she whispered to
Charlotte.

"Hang on, I've got an
idea," Charlotte whispered back. "Would you
really like to go ice skating?" she called to
Holly and Ivy.

"Oh yes!" they both said.

Mia touched her pendant to Charlotte's
once more, making a perfect heart.

"I wish that Holly and Ivy could go ice
skating!" said Charlotte.

FLASH!

This time, light blazed out of the pendants and swirled over the pond.

"Oh, wow!" gasped Holly as the snow on the pond's surface disappeared and fairy lights started twinkling in the trees around them.

The magical light swirled over a nearby

log, and the next instant there were four pairs
of white skates with sparkly laces waiting for
them! The girls ran over to
sit on the log, took off
their boots and put
on the ice skates.
Ivy's skates had two
blades at the bottom
instead of one to help
her balance.

"There are skates for us too!" Mia gasped.
She hadn't been expecting that!

"Hooray!" cried Charlotte, stepping straight
on to the ice. Pushing one foot in front of the
other, she glided across the surface. "Come on
everyone, this is fun!"

Mia grinned as her friend started skating backwards across the pond.

"This is so cool!" cried Holly, following Charlotte on to the ice.

"I love ice skating!" said Ivy. She wobbled a bit and Mia grabbed her hand.

"We can skate together!" she said to the

little girl. Mia loved ice skating, but she wasn't as confident as Charlotte, who could do jumps and spins. Ivy held Mia's hand and they skated round the edge, while Charlotte and Holly whizzed round the middle of the pond.

"This is fun!" cried Ivy. She let go of Mia's hand and sped up, heading towards the centre.

Mia was about to follow her when her eyes caught a flicker of movement in the trees around the pond.

"Faster I say! Faster, you imbecile!"

Mia's heart sank at the sound of the voice. "Charlotte!" she cried in alarm. "Princess Poison is coming!"

But Charlotte was spinning too fast to hear. Just then, a sleigh came out of the trees, pulled by Hex. Princess Poison was in it, reclining on a heap of furs. Hex's face was red and he was puffing and panting.

"Faster!" Princess Poison shrieked. "I need to—" She broke off as she saw the girls. "Aha!" she cried. "We've found them!"

"Go away!" Mia shouted bravely.

Princess Poison stood up in the sleigh. "Oh, I will, but first I'm going to stop you from granting any more wishes. Best of all, if you don't grant a Christmas wish, Christmas at Wishing Star Palace will be ruined too!" she spat.

"Oh no you won't," Mia said, seeing Ivy's eyes start to fill with tears. "We won't let you ruin anyone's Christmas wish."

"Oh, really?" Princess Poison cackled. "I think you'll find you're skating on very thin ice – in every way possible!" She pulled out her wand and pointed it at the girls.

"Pesky girls, joined by your heart,
On the ice you're far apart.
Defying me you will regret,
So here's a lesson you won't forget!"

Green fire hit the ice.

BANG! A sound like a pistol shot rang through the air and the ice started to crack.

Ivy squealed and grabbed Holly's hand.

Princess Poison shrieked with laughter.

"Now, let's see how much you like skating! Toodle-oo!" She waved her wand and she and Hex both vanished.

"The ice's cracking!" cried Holly. "We're going to fall in!"

"Don't worry," Mia called over to them.

"We can use our magic!"

"No we can't!" Charlotte shouted. "You're over there and I'm here. We can't touch our pendants together to make a wish."

Mia realised that Charlotte was right. This time they couldn't use magic.

"Be careful!" Charlotte cried, a horrid chill running down her spine as another long crack appeared in the ice.

"Help!" gasped Holly, clinging on to Ivy as the cracks spread.

Mia looked round desperately. If they fell into the freezing water they'd be in serious trouble. What were they going to do?

CHAPTER TWO
Skating on Thin Ice!

Mia thought fast. She remembered a nature documentary she had once seen about animals that lived in snowy places. Penguins had large, flat feet to spread their weight so the ice was less likely to break when they walked on it. It suddenly gave her an idea.

She grabbed a long tree branch and pushed it out across the ice towards the other girls.

"Lie down and spread your bodies out," she told them. "Try to get hold of the branch and I'll pull you to safety."

Charlotte helped Ivy lie down. "You go first," she said to the little girl, pulling the end of the tree branch towards her. "Hold on tight."

Ivy clung to the branch, looking very pale.

Mia pulled her to the edge of the pond. "She's safe!" she cried, helping Ivy get to her feet.

"You go next," Charlotte said to Holly.

"But what about you?" said Holly.

"I'll be fine," said Charlotte. "Ivy needs you."

Holly lay as flat as she could on the ice and Mia pulled her to safety.

"Now you, Charlotte!" Mia called, her heart pounding as she looked at her best friend stranded in the middle of the pond.

Charlotte reached for the branch, but just then there was another loud crack.

"Charlotte!" Mia screamed as the ice broke into large chunks. Charlotte wobbled dangerously on the piece she was standing on.

Charlotte flung her arms out and got her balance back, but she couldn't reach the branch now.

"Don't worry," she called. "I think I can get across. It'll be just like jumping over some stepping stones!"

"Be careful!" Mia begged.

Charlotte jumped from the ice floe to the

next one. She landed
lightly, and then
jumped again.
Jump by
jump, she
made her way
back to the edge
of the pond.

"I'm so
glad you're
OK," Mia
said, hugging
Charlotte.

"I can't believe Princess Poison did that,"
Charlotte said breathlessly, as they took off
their skates and put their boots back on.

"She's mean, mean, mean!" said Ivy, scowling. "I don't like her at all."

Mia glanced at Charlotte. This wasn't good. Holly and Ivy were both looking miserable. This wasn't the happy Christmas the sisters wanted. Mia knew they couldn't let Princess Poison spoil their wish! "We're all safe now. Why don't we play in the snow?" she said. "Let's make a snowman!"

"I've got an even better idea – how about we make a snow princess?" said Charlotte.

Ivy's face brightened instantly. "Ooh yes, let's do that!"

"First we need to make the body," said Charlotte. "Let's get some snow."

They soon warmed up as they ran about

collecting snow. They gave their snow princess beautiful long hair, a tiara made from some twigs and a skirt decorated with leaves. She looked brilliant!

"What shall we call her?" asked Ivy.

"Princess Alice," said Mia, shooting a look at Charlotte, who grinned and nodded.

"Hey – what do you sing at a snowman's birthday party?" said Charlotte.

The others looked blank.

"*Freeze* a Jolly Good Fellow, of course!" she said with a chuckle.

Ivy giggled. She and Holly were looking much happier now.

Holly checked the time on her phone. "I think we'd better go home soon and get ready for the concert."

"Maybe your dad will there when we get back," said Mia hopefully.

But when they got back Mrs Lee didn't have

good news. "I'm afraid Dad's still delayed," she told Holly and Ivy. "We'll just have to keep our fingers crossed he gets back in time for the concert. You should go and get ready."

Holly and Ivy sadly hurried upstairs to get changed.

"I hope Mr Lee makes it home," Charlotte said to Mia. "Holly and Ivy will be so upset if he doesn't."

"There's still time," said Mia. "But I'm worried Princess Poison will come back and try to ruin things again. And we only have two wishes left."

Charlotte squeezed her hand. "Don't worry. If she does turn up, we'll stop her from doing anything mean."

Mia felt better. With Charlotte beside her she felt like she could do anything. They would stop Princess Poison if she came up with another wicked plan. "We'll make sure that Holly and Ivy have a happy family Christmas!" she declared.

When Holly and Ivy were ready, they all walked to the square where the carol concert was taking place. A man was roasting chestnuts and another was handing out mince pies and mulled wine to the parents. An enormous Christmas tree stood in the centre of the square. Its branches were decorated with fairy lights but they hadn't been lit up yet. Mia remembered Holly had said that would happen after the carols.

Holly and Ivy ran over to where a group were gathering around the choirmaster. "Let's start by warming up your voices," he called.

Mia's eyes caught a flash of green. For one brief second it seemed to light up the choir. Had she imagined it? "Charlotte, did you see that?" she whispered.

"What?" said Charlotte, who was looking round at all the crowds.

"That green light that flashed by the choir," said Mia anxiously.

Charlotte shook her head. "No, but look over there!" She pointed at two figures approaching – one tall and thin, one small and round. They were dressed in big coats and hats with scarves covering their faces. The tall, thin one was wearing pointy, high-heeled boots.

"Do you think that's Princess Poison and Hex?"

Mia's heart began to thump in her chest nervously. "It might be."

"Ready, and after three," called the choirmaster. "One, two, three and ... "

The choir opened their mouths to sing, but instead they all started to make horrible croaking noises.

Holly and Ivy spluttered and coughed as they tried to clear their throats.

"What's happened to you all?" the choirmaster said in dismay.

Charlotte turned to Mia. "Holly and Ivy were singing fine earlier."

"They sound too croaky to sing!" sniggered the small round man.

The tall thin figure beside him laughed gleefully. "Oh, dear. What a shame. Everyone will be so disappointed!"

Mia pulled Charlotte closer. "It *is* them! We've got to do something! This concert's so important to Holly and Ivy. They'll be really upset if Holly can't do her solo."

Charlotte nodded and pulled out her pendant. It was glowing faintly because they'd already used up four wishes. "Let's make another wish – we can't let Princess Poison ruin the concert!"

CHAPTER THREE
Croaky Carols

Mia touched her pendant to Charlotte's.
"I wish the choir would get their voices back!"

There was a flash of light and then both girls gasped as they found themselves carrying two large silver trays. On the trays were mugs of hot chocolate topped with whipped cream and little pink and white marshmallows.

"What are these for?" whispered Mia in

surprise, looking at Charlotte.

"Maybe they'll help the choir sing," said Charlotte. "Try some hot chocolate," she called, carrying her tray over to the choir. "It might soothe your voices."

The choir all took mugs of the hot chocolate, croaking their thanks. There were two mugs left over for Mia and Charlotte.

Mia sipped the hot, creamy drink, warmth spreading through her body and tingling all the way down to her toes.

Then the choir started clearing their throats, their voices returning.

"That was so weird," one girl said.

"My voice just disappeared," said Holly.

"Don't worry," the choirmaster told them. "It must have been the cold air. When you've all finished your hot chocolate then we'll try again."

Mia glanced round and saw Princess Poison glaring at her and Charlotte. "Uh-oh," she said. "I think we've made Princess Poison mad."

"She's making *me* mad," said Charlotte, with a scowl.

The singers put their empty mugs down and got ready to rehearse again. This time they all sang beautifully and the choirmaster looked very pleased at the end. "Excellent!" he told them. He looked around at the crowds of people starting to gather. "Take a short break and then we'll start the concert."

Mia and Charlotte went over to Mrs Lee with Holly and Ivy.

"Have you heard from Dad yet?" Holly asked her mum.

"Yes." Mrs Lee looked anxious. "He's driving back from the airport. He's doing everything he can to get here on time."

Holly and Ivy made their way back to the choirmaster, looking downcast.

"I wish there was something we could do," said Mia. "They want their dad to be here so badly."

Charlotte glanced down at her pendant. It was glowing very faintly. "We have one wish left," she said thoughtfully. "But we'd better use it very carefully."

"Or maybe not!" a voice snapped behind them. "Maybe I have a better idea."

They swung round. Princess Poison and Hex were standing behind them.

"I have a bargain for you," Princess Poison told them haughtily.

Charlotte frowned. "We're not interested!"

Princess Poison's eyebrows raised. "Really? Not even if I said all this Christmassy singing has put me into such a good mood that I want to call a truce?" She gave them a wide toothy smile and turned to Hex. "That's right, isn't it, Hex? I want us all to be friends."

Hex looked surprised. "Do you?" Princess Poison trod on his foot with her pointy boots. "Oh yes … yes," he said hurriedly. "Of course you do."

"So, my dears," Princess Poison purred. "Here's the deal – I'll stop trying to ruin the Secret Princesses' Christmas and in return, you two will stop training to be Secret Princesses."

"What?" Charlotte spluttered.

"No way!" said Mia.

Princess Poison's eyes narrowed. "Think about it, my dears … You could give everyone a lovely Christmas. All I'm asking is that you forget about becoming Secret Princesses." She waved a hand airily. "I mean, who wants to be one of those silly princesses anyway?"

"I do!" said Mia.

"So do I," said Charlotte, nodding hard. "Secret Princesses aren't silly. Training to become one and getting to see Mia is the best thing ever!"

Princess Poison's frown deepened. "If you don't agree to my offer, I'll make you and all your friends very sorry indeed."

"Forget it! We're never going to agree!" Charlotte told her.

Princess Poison's eyes flashed icily. "Well, don't say I didn't warn you ..." She whipped out her wand and chanted a spell.

**"Snowflakes fall, street lights fail,
Winds blow up into a gale!"**

Snow started to swirl down and a gust of wind blew Mia's hair into her face.

"Your friends' father won't get to the concert now," hissed Princess Poison. "And it's all your fault. If you'd made a deal with me, it could have been very different. You could have made your friends so happy. That will teach you to mess with me!"

Grabbing Hex, she vanished.

Mia looked up at the swirling snow. "What are we going to do?" she said in dismay. "Now Mr Lee will never get here in time and the girls won't have their happy family Christmas!"

As tree branches swayed in the strong wind, snow fell more heavily, building up on the pavement and roads. The choir gathered closer together, determinedly singing *Rudolph the*

Red Nosed Reindeer. Mia saw Holly and Ivy exchange anxious looks. She was sure they were thinking about their dad.

"This is awful," she said. "It must be almost impossible to drive now."

"I wonder how Santa manages it," said Charlotte glumly. "He always manages to fly his sleigh, no matter what the weather's like."

"Rudolph!" Mia gasped, listening to the song the choir was singing. "Santa uses his glowing red nose to help him see."

Charlotte frowned. "How's that going to help? I don't think we can wish for Mr Lee to have a red nose!"

Despite feeling anxious, Mia couldn't help giggling. "No, silly! We need to find something that shines so bright that Mr Lee can see it through the snow and find his way here." Her eyes fell on the dark Christmas tree. "And I know just what!"

CHAPTER FOUR
A Guiding Light

Mia held out her pendant. Charlotte didn't waste time asking any questions – she just brought her pendant to meet Mia's.

"I wish to light up the square with Christmas lights!" said Mia.

Sparkling light shot out of their pendants and streamed around the square. As it touched the Christmas tree's branches, there was a flare

of gold and all the fairy lights suddenly started to shine. At the same time, Christmas lights shone out all around the rest of the square too.

The crowd gasped. The choir faltered for a moment, but the choirmaster kept conducting and they sang on. The square looked wonderful, with all the lights twinkling in the dark night.

I hope this works, thought Mia.

The choir came to the end of *Rudolph the Red Nosed Reindeer* and started their second song: *Silent Night.* Charlotte caught her breath as the music started. "This is the song with Holly's solo," she realised.

Mia's eyes scanned the road leading up to the square. Suddenly, she saw a car's

headlights in the distance. The car stopped
and a man jumped out. He hurried through the
snow, pulling his coat around him as the choir
reached the first chorus.

"Do you think that's Mr Lee?" Mia said, her
heart lifting with hope.

"Daddy!" Ivy cried in delight.

"I think so!" Charlotte said with a grin.

The man waved. Ivy jumped up and down,
beaming and waving back. Holly was too
grown-up to call out to her dad, but Mia
and Charlotte saw her smile and give him
a tiny wave.

The snow stopped falling and the wind died
down as Holly's voice rang out, pure and sweet
as she reached the high notes effortlessly.

Her singing carried across the square. Mr Lee reached his wife and wrapped an arm around her shoulders. Together they stood, smiling proudly as Holly sang her solo.

"He got here just in time!" said Mia, breathing out in relief.

"Holly and Ivy look so pleased," said Charlotte, tucking her arm through Mia's. "We did it. We made them all happy."

The girls rested their heads together as they listened to the Christmas songs and then joined in as everyone sang the final song, *We Wish You a Merry Christmas.* As soon as the concert was over, Holly and Ivy raced over to their parents.

"Daddy! You got here!" Ivy cried. Mr Lee swung her round, then he hugged Holly.

"I thought I wasn't going to make it," he said. "I was pretty close to the square when it suddenly got really dark and snow started falling heavily. But then I saw all the lights shining. They guided me to you."

"This is going to be the best Christmas ever," said Holly. "Because we're all together as a family!"

There was a sudden magical chiming of bells and the lights around the square shone even brighter, changing colours in a brilliant, beautiful display.

"Holly and Ivy's wish has been granted," Charlotte whispered to Mia in delight.

Mia pointed up to the sky. High above, one of the stars twinkled brighter than all the others. "I bet that's Wishing Star Palace, shining out to let us know we did it," said Mia.

"Pah!" a voice spat behind them. They swung round and saw Princess Poison.

"I can still ruin their Christmas," she gloated.

"You've used all your wishes up now, but I still have my magic. I can spoil their turkey, steal their presents, ruin their pudding … "

"That won't make any difference!" Charlotte interrupted, stepping forward and folding her arms. "Yes, you could do those things, but it won't matter. Christmas is about being with the people you love.

Holly and Ivy won't care if anything else goes wrong."

"Charlotte's right," said Mia. "Their family will have a special Christmas no matter what happens, because they've got each other."

"You really don't know anything about Christmas, do you, Princess Poison?" said Charlotte, waving her hand at the square. People were smiling, laughing and hugging as they exchanged Christmas greetings. "You should stick around – you might find the Christmas spirit is catching!"

"Catching!" A look of horror crossed Princess Poison's face.

Hex backed away hastily.

"Let's go!" Princess Poison snapped at him.

She started to run away, but her high-heeled boots slipped on the snow and she fell over.

Some people tried to help her up, but she batted their hands away. "Get off me! Go away!" she cried. "I don't want to catch your Christmas spirit!"

Scrambling to her feet, she slipped and slid across the snowy square with Hex hurrying after her.

Just then, Mia and Charlotte heard their names being called. Princess Ella, wearing a warm winter coat, came through the crowd towards them. "Well done, girls," she said softly, putting her arms around their shoulders. "We're all very proud of you."

Mrs Lee glanced over in their direction. Seeing Ella with them she smiled and waved.

"It's time to say goodbye to your new friends now," Princess Ella whispered to the girls.

They all went over to the Lee family. Ivy greeted them with a big grin. "Look! Daddy got back in time!"

"Santa made our wish come true," said
Holly. She gave Charlotte and Mia a smile.
"But he had some help from his elves."

"Thank you for having Charlotte and Mia
over this afternoon," Ella said to Mrs Lee.

"It was no problem at all." Mrs Lee gave
them a warm look. "Have a great Christmas!"

"You too," said Charlotte.

Ivy hugged them. "I hope your Christmas wishes are granted, too," she whispered in Mia's ear.

Mia and Charlotte waved goodbye and headed off to a quiet corner of the square with Ella. "Are you ready for some more magic?" Ella asked.

"Oh yes!" they breathed.

"Hold hands then," Ella whispered, pulling out her wand and waving it. "Because we're going back to Wishing Star Palace!"

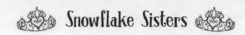

Charlotte and Mia grasped hands and felt themselves being lifted up into the air and whisked away through the stars!

CHAPTER FIVE
The Best Christmas Ever!

Charlotte and Mia landed back in the hall at Wishing Star Palace, where the Secret Princesses were gathered around the Christmas tree. They were all wearing beautiful velvet gowns with fur trim.

"Oh, girls, you did so well," said Alice.

"We were so relieved when Princess Ella turned up in the shop!" said Charlotte.

Alice grinned. "Yes, we realised you might need a bit of help!"

"We saw Princess Poison try to make a bargain with you," said Princess Sylvie. "We were very glad you didn't agree."

"We never would!" said Charlotte. "We love training to be Secret Princesses."

"It feels so good to make people happy," said Mia. "We would never want to give that up."

"You made Holly and Ivy's Christmas wish come true," said Princess Ella. "And that means there's plenty of Christmas magic here at Wishing Star Palace!"

"You've arrived back just in time for presents," said Princess Sylvie, taking their hands. "Because we all like to spend Christmas day with our families, we have a special Secret Princess party just before Christmas."

Alice went over to the fireplace, where there was a massive knitted stocking hanging from the mantel. "Our presents are in here," she said. She looked round. "Now that everyone's here, should we start?"

All the princesses nodded eagerly, and
one by one they went up to the stocking and
pulled out a present. The stocking magically
gave each princess
the perfect
present.
Princess
Sophie's
present was
a new set of
paintbrushes,
Princess Sylvie
had a new
kitchen
whisk,
Princess Ella had

a calendar with cute pictures of puppies, and Alice had a new microphone. Finally, it was Charlotte and Mia's turn.

Mia held her breath as she reached into the stocking and felt around for a present. She drew out a box wrapped in glittery silver paper and tied with turquoise ribbon. She opened it and gasped with delight as she found a beautiful baking set with lots of fun biscuit cutters.

Charlotte opened her present next, and got a book of jokes.

"Hooray!" she said happily. "Now I can tell even more jokes!"

Mia groaned.

Charlotte nudged her. "You're pleased, really. I know you are!"

As the girls laughed, Alice went over to the Christmas tree. "Charlotte and Mia, because you were both so brilliant today, we've decided that you should have an early Christmas present."

Princess Sophie nodded. "Our Christmas celebration would have been ruined if it wasn't for you. So we want to give you something really special to thank you."

Alice took the half-heart glass baubles off the tree and gave one to each girl. "These are magic. You can use them to each make a Christmas wish of your own."

Mia looked at the beautiful bauble. "I don't know what to wish for," she said. "I've just had an amazing adventure with my best friend. There's nothing else I could possibly want."

Charlotte smiled. "I feel exactly the same."

Alice looked from one girl to the other. "Really? Surely there must be something else you'd like to wish for."

Mia looked at Charlotte and realised that deep down she *did* have another wish. "The only thing I wish is that we could spend Christmas together. That would be the best Christmas ever ... but that can't happen."

"It would be awesome," said Charlotte. "That's my wish too. But it's impossible."

For a brief second, a beautiful light flashed through the baubles.

"Remember, nothing's impossible with Christmas magic," said Alice, smiling. "You'll just have to wait and see if your wish comes true. It's time for you both to go home now."

"Merry Christmas!" called the princesses as Charlotte and Mia hugged goodbye.

"I hope we see each other again very soon," Charlotte told Mia.

"Something tells me you will," Alice said with a knowing wink. She waved her wand and a cloud of red and green sparkles surrounded the girls and swept them away.

Mia landed back in her bedroom with her new baking set on her knee. She rubbed her hands over her face. It was hard to believe that a moment ago she'd been opening presents with the Secret Princesses. It had been their most incredible adventure yet, and best of all they had helped make Holly and Ivy's wish come true.

She heard footsteps on the landing outside her room. She looked up, expecting to see Elsie running in with a card, but instead her mum looked round her door. "Mia! I've just had some incredible news! Charlotte's mum emailed me to say they've decided Christmas won't be the same in the sun, so they've booked some last-minute flights back to England. I've invited them to stay with us for Christmas!"

"Really?" Mia gasped, jumping to her feet.

"Yes. It'll be a squeeze, but I think we'll have a very merry Christmas this year!"

Mia hugged her mum tightly. As she did, she looked out of the window and saw a star twinkling extra brightly in the sky. "Thank you," she whispered to all the princesses at

Wishing Star Palace. She remembered what Alice had said – with Christmas magic anything really *is* possible!

The End

Join Charlotte and Mia in their next Secret Princesses adventure!

Read on for a sneak peek!

Puppy Magic

"One ... two ... three ..." Charlotte Williams counted the seconds as she stood in a perfect handstand, her toes pointing up towards the bright blue sky. The short, dry grass was warm under her fingers and she could smell the sweet oranges ripening on the trees in the back yard. Her brown curls brushed the ground. "Four ... five ... six ..."

"Charlotte!" Mrs Williams opened the back door. "I'm just talking to Mia's mum on the computer. Do you want to come and have a chat with Mia?"

"Of course!" Charlotte's feet touched the grass. Leaping up, she ran over to her mum. "It's ages since I spoke to her!"

Mrs Williams's eyes twinkled. "You mean three whole days."

Charlotte grinned. "That's ages for me and Mia!" She and Mia were best friends. They used to live in the same village in England, until Charlotte's family had moved to California. Although Charlotte had made lots of new friends in America, no one would ever replace Mia.

She hurried inside to the study. The air conditioning was on, keeping the house lovely and cool. When Charlotte had first moved to California she'd found it strange being able to wear shorts every day.

Mia was on the computer screen. Her long, blonde hair was tied back in two plaits and she was wearing pyjamas and her dressing gown. Seeing Charlotte, she waved happily.

Happiness fizzed through Charlotte as she sat down in the office chair. "Hi! What have you been up to?"

"Just normal weekend stuff," said Mia. "We went for a bike ride this morning and then I went to see my Auntie Marie and helped take her dogs for a walk. How about you?"

"I went to a baseball game with Liam and Harvey," said Charlotte.

Just then, a little girl with blonde hair popped her head over Mia's shoulder. It was

Elsie, Mia's younger sister. "Hello, Charlotte!
I can ride my bike without stabilisers now."

"Wow! Well done, Elsie," said Charlotte.

"Are Mia and Elsie there?" Liam and
Harvey, Charlotte's six-year-old twin
brothers, came barrelling into the study. "Hi,
Mia! Hi, Elsie!" they shouted.

"Look, we lost our front teeth!" said Liam,
opening his mouth in front of the computer's
camera to show them that one of his front
teeth had fallen out.

"You've got matching gaps!" said Mia as
Harvey pointed to his mouth too.

"Come on, boys," Mrs Williams said,
coming into the room. "Leave Charlotte and
Mia to have a chat. It might be lunchtime

here, but it's evening in England and Mia will probably have to go to bed soon."

Mia waved goodbye to the twins and then persuaded Elsie to go and play.

Finally, she and Charlotte were able to chat uninterrupted. They caught up about school and everything else they'd been doing until Mia's mum broke into the conversation. "Time to say goodbye and go to bed, Mia!" she called. "You can chat again soon."

Charlotte touched the half-heart pendant she wore around her neck. "Hopefully *very* soon," she said, winking at Mia.

Mia held up her own matching pendant. "Oh, yes," she said, winking back.

Charlotte felt a warm glow in her tummy.

She and Mia shared the most amazing secret. When she had moved to America, their old babysitter, Alice, had given them both magic necklaces!

Whenever the necklaces started to glow, Mia and Charlotte were whisked away to an incredibly beautiful palace in the clouds. The first time Charlotte and Mia had arrived at Wishing Star Palace, Alice had explained that they'd been chosen to train as Secret Princesses – special girls who used magic to grant people's wishes! Charlotte loved everything about training to be a Secret Princess. It meant she got to do magic – and best of all, have adventures with Mia!

Squeezing the pendant in her fingers,

Charlotte thought longingly, *Oh, I wish we could go to Wishing Star Palace now*. On their last adventure, she and Mia had passed the first stage of their training and earned gorgeous diamond tiaras that they could wear whenever they visited the palace. Now, for the second stage of their training, they needed to help four more people. If they did, they'd earn sparkling ruby princess slippers that would let them travel by magic. It was all so exciting!

Charlotte saw light flicker across the surface of her pendant. She caught her breath and peered closer. Was she imagining it? No – the pendant was starting to glow!

Charlotte looked at Mia, who was staring

at her own necklace. It was glowing too! The girls grinned at each other, then Charlotte shut the laptop and ran to her bedroom, her heart racing. No time would pass while she was away, but she still didn't want her family to see her magically vanish! Shutting the door behind her, she opened her fingers. The magic pendant was now glowing like a ray of sunshine.

"I wish I could see Mia at Wishing Star Palace!" Charlotte whispered.

Light blazed out, surrounding her. She felt it swirl around her and lift her up and away. Excitement flashed through Charlotte. Another Secret Princess adventure was just about to begin!

Charlotte's feet came to rest on velvety soft grass. She opened her eyes and saw that she was standing in front of Wishing Star Palace. Flags flew from its four turrets, ivy climbed up its marble walls, and its heart-shaped windows glinted in the sunlight.

"Yay!" cried Charlotte, twirling on the spot. The long, pink princess dress she'd magically changed into swished around her legs. Putting a hand up to her head, she smiled as she felt her diamond tiara in her brown curls.

"Charlotte!" Mia peeked out from behind a nearby tree with pink candyfloss and candy canes hanging from its branches. She was wearing a beautiful golden dress with silver

embroidery and her own diamond tiara
nestled in her blonde hair.

They ran to meet each other and hugged.

"It's so brilliant to see you," said Mia. "I
mean, it's great talking on the computer but
it's even better to be together for real!"

Charlotte knew just what she meant.
She was so happy she felt like turning ten
cartwheels in a row but she knew it might be
tricky in her long dress. "The palace looks
great, doesn't it?" she said, shading her eyes
and looking at the glittering turrets.

When they had first come to Wishing
Star Palace, it had looked very different.
Princess Poison, a Secret Princess who had
turned bad, had put a spell on the palace.

With every wish she ruined, instead of granting, she'd made the palace crumble and break. But by granting four people's wishes, Mia and Charlotte had helped mend the palace, and earned their princess tiaras.

"It looks so much better," agreed Mia. She looked towards the doorway. "Should we see if anyone is inside?"

Read *Puppy Magic* to find out what happens next!

Christmas Paper Chains

Materials
- Coloured paper
- Glue or sticky tape
- Scissors

Steps

1. Cut the paper into strips about 2cm wide by 20cm long. It doesn't matter if they're not perfect.

2. Take one strip of paper and curl it around so that the two ends meet. Glue one end to the other and hold for several seconds until it's dry. Or you can use sticky tape instead.

3. Put the next strip of paper through the middle of your first chain link. Curl the ends of the second strip together until they meet and then glue or tape that one too.

4. Do this over and over again until the chain is as long as you want.

5. Use your Christmas paper chain to decorate your room and make it feel really Christmassy!

Princess Sylvie's Gingerbread Recipe:

Makes about twenty biscuits in gingerbread man shape. Why not decorate them so that they look just like you?

Ingredients

- 2 tsp ground ginger
- 1 tsp bicarbonate of soda
- 350g plain flour
- 100g butter
- 175g soft light brown sugar
- 1 egg
- 4 tbsp golden syrup
- A spoonful of magic (only available at Wishing Star Palace)

Steps

1. Get an adult to preheat the oven to 190°C/Gas Mark 5

2. Sieve the flour into a bowl and add the bicarbonate of soda and the ginger

3. Use your fingers to rub in the butter

4. Add the sugar and stir in the egg and syrup to make a firm dough

5. Put the gingerbread dough on a lightly floured surface

6. Roll out to about 5mm thick and cut out your gingerbread men

7. You can make gingerbread people or any shape you like – they'll taste just as yummy!

8. Put a sheet of baking paper on a tray and lay out the biscuits. Make sure you leave lots of room because the gingerbread can spread

9. Bake for 10-15 minutes until golden brown

10. As soon as they're cool, decorate them with icing!

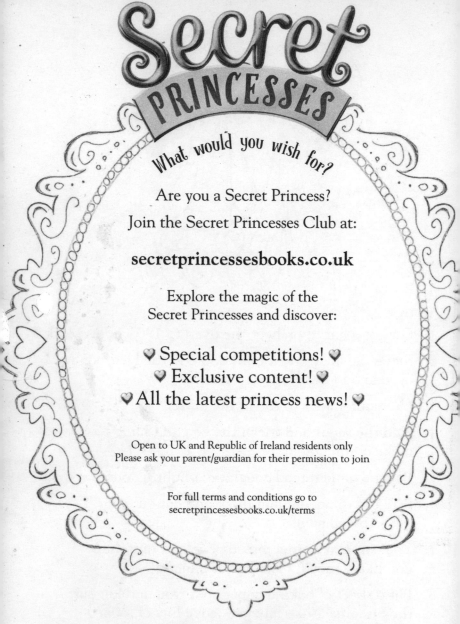

Secret PRINCESSES

What would you wish for?

Are you a Secret Princess?

Join the Secret Princesses Club at:

secretprincessesbooks.co.uk

Explore the magic of the
Secret Princesses and discover:

♥ Special competitions! ♥
♥ Exclusive content! ♥
♥ All the latest princess news! ♥

Open to UK and Republic of Ireland residents only
Please ask your parent/guardian for their permission to join

For full terms and conditions go to
secretprincessesbooks.co.uk/terms

Snowflake1

Enter the special code above on the website to receive

50 Princess Points